HELPING YOUR BRAND-NEW READER

Here's how to make first-time reading easy and fun:

◗ Read the introduction at the beginning of each story aloud. Look through the pictures together so that your child can see what happens in the story before reading the words.

◗ Read one or two pages to your child, placing your finger under each word.

◗ Let your child touch the words and read the rest of the story. Give him or her time to figure out each new word.

◗ If your child gets stuck on a word, you might say, *"Try something. Look at the picture. What would make sense?"*

◗ If your child is still stuck, supply the right word. This will allow him or her to continue to read and enjoy the story. You might say, *"Could this word be 'ball'?"*

◗ Always praise your child. Praise what he or she reads correctly, and praise good tries too.

◗ Give your child lots of chances to read the story again and again. The more your child reads, the more confident he or she will become.

◗ Have fun!

First edition 2013

Library of Congress Catalog Card Number 2012954467

ISBN 978-0-7636-6655-2

13 14 15 16 17 18 SWT 10 9 8 7 6 5 4 3 2 1

Printed in Dongguan, Guangdong, China

This book was typeset in Arta Medium.
The illustrations were created digitally.

Candlewick Press
99 Dover Street
Somerville, Massachusetts 02144

visit us at www.candlewick.com

Here Comes Super Grover!

ILLUSTRATED BY **Ernie Kwiat**

CANDLEWICK PRESS

Contents

Super Grover to the Rescue

Introduction

This story is called *Super Grover to the Rescue*. It's about how Elmo tries to get his wagon down the stairs, and Super Grover helps him!

3

Elmo has a wagon.

4

He sees the steps. Oh, no!

Super Grover brings a balloon.

6

"A balloon won't work," says Elmo.

Super Grover brings a kite.

"A kite won't work," says Elmo.

Super Grover brings a board.

Elmo walks down the ramp!

Super Grover and the Rock

Introduction

This story is called *Super Grover and the Rock*. It's about how Super Grover tries to move a rock from his garden.

13

Super Grover sees a big rock.

He tries to sweep the rock.

15

He tries to push the rock.

He tries to pull the rock.

Super Grover gets a smaller rock.

He gets a shovel.

The rock moves!

"Hey!" says Bert.

Super Grover's Basket

Introduction

This story is called *Super Grover's Basket.*
It's about how Cookie Monster and Super
Grover use a basket and a rope to carry
snacks to their tree house!

Cookie Monster puts cookies in a basket.

Super Grover pulls the basket up.

He lowers the basket down.

Cookie puts milk in the basket.

Super Grover pulls the basket up.

He lowers the basket down.

Super Grover pulls and pulls.

"Cookie Monster!" says Super Grover.

Super Grover and the Bike

Introduction

This story is called *Super Grover and the Bike.* It's about how Super Grover helps Abby find the right wheel for her bike!

Abby's bike has just one big wheel.

34

"Try this!" says Super Grover.

"That is a square," says Abby.

36

"Try this!" says Super Grover.

"That is a triangle," says Abby.

Elmo brings a round wheel.

Now Abby's bike has two big wheels.

Abby rides the bike.